Inside MY Mind

A Book About Me!

By Suzanne Francis

Illustrated by the Disney Storybook Art Team

Random House 🏠 New York

rhcbooks.com

ISBN 978-0-7364-3286-3 (trade)

MANUFACTURED IN CHINA

10 9 8 7 6 5 4 3

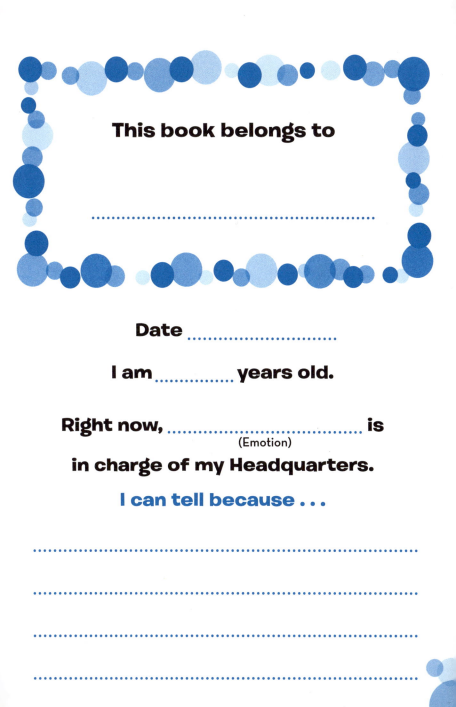

This book belongs to

....

Date ....

I am .... years old.

Right now, ... is
(Emotion)
in charge of my Headquarters.

I can tell because . . .

....

....

....

....

Meet **RILEY....**

RILEY

"Pretty much everyone in my family skates. It's kind of a family tradition. We go out on the lake almost every weekend."

Riley is an eleven-year-old girl who has just moved from Minnesota to San Francisco with her mom and dad. As she struggles to adjust to her new home, Riley's happy personality starts to fade.

Meet Riley's **EMOTIONS....**

JOY

"We are going to have a good day, which will turn into a good week, which will turn into a good year, which turns into a good LIFE!"

As Riley's lead Emotion, Joy's job is to help Riley live a happy life. Joy has an incredible knack for always finding the fun.

SADNESS

"Crying helps me slow down and obsess over the weight of life's problems."

If Riley feels dark and gloomy, Sadness is there. Sure, she's a bit of a downer, but no one is better at helping Riley cry it out or get a comforting hug from Mom and Dad.

ANGER

"GrrrrrrraaaaaaaaAAHHHHHHHHH!"

In a world full of injustices, Anger tries to help Riley get treated fairly. He may be short, but Anger's frustrations are BIG.

FEAR

"All right, we did not die today! I call that an unqualified success."

Fear can't help seeing the dangerous and scary—there is so much of it everywhere! Fear helps Riley navigate life's hazards, from power cords to roller skates.

DISGUST

"That is the most disgusting thing I have ever seen."

Disgust alerts Riley whenever there is something potentially disgusting around, to protect her from being poisoned—both physically and socially.

Meet Riley's
IMAGINARY FRIEND....

BING BONG

"I'm mostly cotton candy, but shape-wise, I'm part cat, part elephant, and part dolphin."

Bing Bong was Riley's imaginary friend when she was three. He wishes they could play together again—they were supposed to take his rocket to the moon!

Are you READY?

Grab a pen or a pencil and join Riley and her Emotions on a journey inside *your* mind!

CHAPTER 1
Joy

Imagine Joy

Joy is all about happiness. What would life be like if Joy was your lead Emotion?

If Joy were in charge of my Headquarters . . .

....

....

....

....

....

....

....

....

....

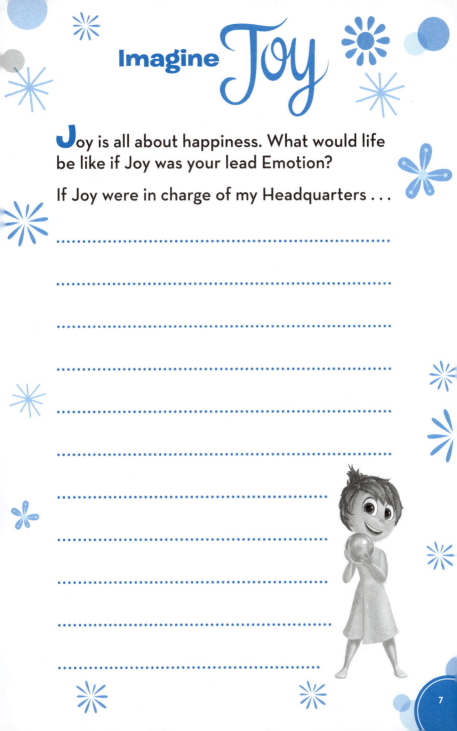

Inside **JOY'S** Head

What is Joy thinking right now?
Fill in the thought bubble below.

Happy **BABY** Memories

Joy loves remembering Riley as a baby.
What might the Emotions inside your
Headquarters see when they look at a memory
sphere from when you were a baby?

**Draw a picture of your baby memory
inside the sphere.**

The Daily SCOOP

Date ....

Every day is full of Emotions.

Write about all the things that made you joyful, sad, angry, scared, and grossed out today.

JOYFUL Things

....

....

....

....

SAD Things

....

....

....

....

ANGRY Things

....

....

....

....

SCARY Things

....

....

....

....

GROSS Things

....

....

....

....

DREAM Star

There are many characters who play a part in Riley's dreams, but some "stars" have recurring roles. Rainbow Unicorn is Joy's favorite star of Riley's dreams. Who is your favorite star of your dreams?

Draw a picture here.

Write about something your favorite star has done in your dreams lately.

....

....

....

....

....

....

....

....

....

....

....

....

....

CHEERLEADER!

Joy tries to bring cheer to Riley every day. How have you cheered someone up?

....

....

Who has cheered you up lately?

....

....

What did they do to cheer you up?

....

....

What are some things you do to cheer yourself up?

....

....

....

Draw a picture of yourself when you are happy.

A **CLEAN** Slate

Joy believes that "an empty room is an opportunity!" Decorate this room to make it look like somewhere you'd love to live.

Finding the FUN

Joy says, "You can't focus on what's going wrong. There's always a way to turn things around and find the fun."

Write about a time when things weren't going well at first but then you found the fun.

I remember when things weren't going so well . . .

....

....

....

....

Then I found the fun because . . .

....

....

....

....

Travel GAMES

Joy thinks car trips are a great excuse to play travel games! Here are some that you can play when you're on the road. These games require two or more players, so hopefully you have some other people looking for fun in the car!

Name That Tune

All you need for this game is a quiet car and your melodious voice! Think of a song and don't tell anyone what it is. Hum it and see who can name that tune!

20 Questions

First, pick a category. (Categories can be things like Animals, Food, or Things at the Beach.) The first answerer thinks of something that falls under the chosen category. Everyone else is a questioner. Questioners take turns asking yes-or-no questions, such as: "Is it big?" "Does it smell bad?" "Can I eat it?" Players can ask up to 20 yes-or-no questions. The questioner who guesses correctly becomes the next answerer!

Backseat Bingo

What You Need:
Bingo cards
Pencils or pens

What You Do:
1. First, make the Bingo cards. It's a good idea to make the cards before the trip so you're ready!
2. In the boxes on the cards, write things you might see on the road, such as a bus, a train, a tractor, deer, or a purple car.
3. Give each player a card and a pencil so they can mark when they spot any of the things on their card.
4. The first person to fill in a row yells "Bingo!" (Even if you're playing solo, don't be afraid to say "Bingo!" It's part of the fun.)
5. Erase the marks on the cards or use new cards and play again.

Alphabet City

Go through the alphabet and try to spot something that starts with each letter. For example, a cornfield would work for the letter "C" and a garage would work for the letter "G." Let's just hope by the time you get to "X" you see a . . . xylophone?

My MIND World

Date ....

Today .... is in charge of my Headquarters.
(Emotion)
I can tell because . . .

....

....

I think .... tried to take over at one point,
(Emotion)

because . . .

....

....

But then things changed when . . .

....

....

and .... took control.
(Emotion)

DOUBLE the Joy!

Which two pictures of Joy are exactly alike?

A

B

C

D

E

F

See page 118 for the answer.

HAPPY Word Search

The following is a list of nine things that make Riley very happy. Look up, down, across, diagonally, and backward in the puzzle below. Can you find all nine words?

clouds	fort	hockey
dessert	French fries	skating
family	friends	trophies

```
F D F G B V D W G J K Z X C V
B O B F D E H C V S W O P N M
L K R V X F R O N C H F R G H
G L O T S A N B C P G F H J Y
N M I R W M H V L K F D G Y T
I N U E E I Y C K O E L F T R
T B Y S R L T X J I D Y F R E
A V T S T Y R U H U F S R D T
K C G E Y K E Z O Y D S I S G
S X B D U M W Q G U G D E C T
I Z S N I N Q W O T C F N W P
U A X W O B A L R R W G D P R
Y Q F R E N C H F R I E S X U
T W O M P V Z A D E Q H F S J
R E L K L C X S E I H P O R T
```

See page 118 for the answer.

Jump for JOY!

Draw some of the things that make you feel joyful.

Make a JAR OF JOY

Write all the things that make you happy on little slips of paper. Then fold the slips and put them in a jar. Whenever you're feeling blue, pull one out to remember the joy!

PUZZLED in Headquarters

Can you find where each puzzle piece belongs in the picture of Headquarters below?

A

B

C

D

E

See page 118 for the answer.

Memory Dump MAZE Madness

Help Joy and Bing Bong find their way out of the Memory Dump!

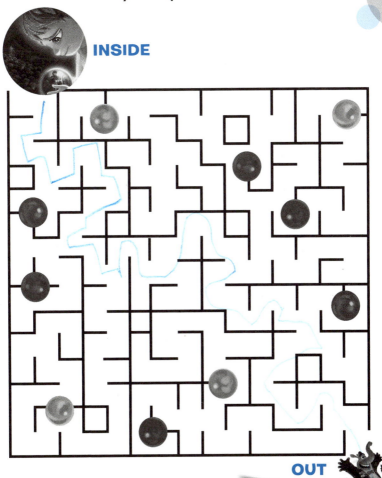

INSIDE

OUT

See page 118 for the answer.

CHAPTER 2
Sadness

Sadness in Charge

Sadness can't help seeing the downside of life.

If Sadness were in charge of my Headquarters for a day . . .

....

....

....

....

....

....

....

....

....

Sad, Sadder, and SADDEST

A scoop of ice cream falling off its cone makes Riley really sad. Make a list of the things that make you sad.

1. ....

2. ....

3. ....

4. ....

5. ....

6. ....

7. ....

8. ....

9. ....

10. ....

Sad MEMORIES

One of Sadness's favorite memories is the time when Riley and her hockey team, the Prairie Dogs, lost the big playoff game. Riley missed the winning shot and felt awful. She even wanted to quit. But because Riley felt sad, her parents and teammates came to cheer her up.

Write about one of your memories that started sad but ended happy.

TWO Sides of the Story

Sadness and Joy have very different perspectives on the things that happen in Riley's life.

Write a story inspired by the scene on the next page from Joy's perspective. Then write the same story from Sadness's perspective. Don't forget to write a title for each story!

Joy's Version

Title: _____

....

....

....

....

....

....

Sadness's Version

Title: _____

....

....

....

....

....

....

The **BLUES**

Sadness turns memory spheres blue when she touches them. Try this activity and turn something blue!

What You Need:
Celery
A knife
Water
A jar or drinking glass
Blue food coloring
A spoon

What You Do:

1. Fill a jar or drinking glass about halfway with water.

2. Squeeze enough blue food coloring into the water to make it turn a nice, deep shade of blue. (About 10 to 15 drops should do it.) Give the water a stir to check your color.

What else can you turn BLUE?

Try the same experiment with a white carnation. How long does it take for the carnation to turn blue?

3. Ask an adult to help trim about one inch off the bottom of the celery stalks. (That's the end without the leaves.)

4. Put the celery stalks into the blue water so that the leaves are sticking out of the jar or glass.

5. Here comes the tough part—waiting! Let the celery sit in the jar or glass overnight. The longer you leave the celery in the water, the bluer it will get.

Please do not eat the blue celery! That would make Disgust very unhappy.

LISTENING Skills

After Bing Bong's wagon rocket is thrown into the Memory Dump, Sadness makes him feel better by listening and comforting him.

Write about a time when you helped a friend who was sad.

....

....

....

....

....

....

....

....

....

....

....

It's RAINING!

Why does Sadness like the rain?

Use the decoder to find the answer.

1	2	3	4	5	6	7	8	9
M	K	I	E	A	R	T	S	Y

10	11	12	13	14	15	16	17	18
V	N	G	H	F	D	O	P	L

$$\frac{\quad}{3}\ \frac{\quad}{7}$$

$$\frac{\quad}{1}\ \frac{\quad}{5}\ \frac{\quad}{2}\ \frac{\quad}{4}\ \frac{\quad}{8}$$

$$\frac{\quad}{4}\ \frac{\quad}{10}\ \frac{\quad}{4}\ \frac{\quad}{6}\ \frac{\quad}{9}\ \frac{\quad}{7}\ \frac{\quad}{13}\ \frac{\quad}{3}\ \frac{\quad}{11}\ \frac{\quad}{12}$$

$$\frac{\quad}{14}\ \frac{\quad}{4}\ \frac{\quad}{4}\ \frac{\quad}{18}$$

$$\frac{\quad}{15}\ \frac{\quad}{6}\ \frac{\quad}{16}\ \frac{\quad}{16}\ \frac{\quad}{17}\ \frac{\quad}{9}.$$

See page 119 for the answer.

The **SHADOW** of Sadness

Which shadow below matches **Sadness's** shadow exactly?

1

2

3

4

5

6

See page 119 for the answer.

Escape from
ABSTRACT THOUGHT!

Help Joy, Sadness, and Bing Bong find their way out of Abstract Thought!

START

EXIT

See page 119 for the answer.

VIEW from Sadness

What is Sadness thinking?
Fill in the thought bubble below.

CORE Memories

Riley's core memories are the memories that run her Islands of Personality. They are the most important memories and are created when Riley has a really big life moment. For example, the first time Riley scored a hockey goal is one of her core memories. That memory powers Hockey Island.

Write about one of your core memories here.

Which of your Islands of Personality do you think that core memory powers?

What's Your *Inside Out* I.Q.?

Choose a word from the word bank to fit into each sentence.

Word Bank:

cloud	fun
crying	listener
dog	memory
foot	shortcut

1. Joy and Sadness have the same favorite _____.

2. Sadness does not know how to find the _____.

3. Joy has to drag Sadness by her _____ through Long Term Memory.

4. Sadness tries to get away from Joy by flying on top of a _____.

5. Joy and Sadness dress up as a _____ to try to wake up Riley.

6. _____ helps Sadness slow down and obsess over life's problems.

7. Sadness does not think she and Joy should take Bing Bong's _____.

8. Sadness is a very good _____.

40   *See page 119 for the answers.*

TEARS of Sadness

With a friend, take turns drawing a line to connect two teardrops below. When a line you draw completes a box, give yourself one point.
If Sadness is in the box, give yourself two points.
When no more boxes can be made, the player with more points wins.

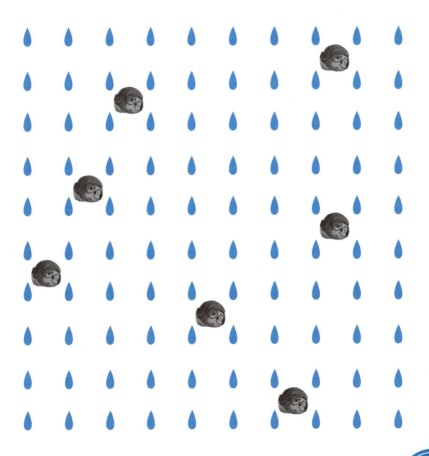

FORGET 'EM

The Forgetters in Long Term Memory vacuum up old memories that Riley doesn't care about anymore, like the names of every Cutie Pie Princess doll. Those memories go to the Memory Dump, and they never come back.

Make a list of some memories you would like to clear out of your mind and send to the dump.

1. ....

2. ....

3. ....

4. ....

5. ....

6. ....

The Forgetters think it's funny to send the memory of a Tripledent gum commercial up to Headquarters for no reason at all. They just like to get the jingle stuck in Riley's head.

Write about a recurring memory that pops into your head.

....

....

....

....

....

....

....

....

....

....

Chapter 3

ANGER

ANGER in COMMAND

If Anger were the lead Emotion in my Headquarters . . .

....

....

....

....

....

....

....

....

....

....

....

It Really **BURNS** Me Up

There isn't enough paper in the world to list all the things that make Anger angry.

Make a list of the things that make you angry.

1. ....

2. ....

3. ....

4. ....

5. ....

6. ....

7. ....

8. ....

9. ....

10. ....

A PORTRAIT of Anger

When Anger gets **REALLY** angry, flames come out of his head!

Draw a picture of what happens to you when you get really angry.

REFLECTIONS of Anger

What is Anger thinking?
Fill in the thought bubble below.

Pizza Destroyer
CRYPTOGRAM

Crack the code to discover who Anger blames for ruining pizza. The numbers below each space correspond to the letters of the alphabet. One letter is filled in to get you started.

Hint: Make a numbered list of the alphabet to help you crack the code!

_ A _ A _ _   A _ _   _ A _
8 1 23 1 9 9 1 14 4 19 1 14

_ _ A _ _ _ _ _ _
6 18 1 14 3 9 19 3 15

See page 119 for the answer.

49

Great **IDEAS!**

The Emotions use idea bulbs to put an idea into Riley's mind. Fill in the following bulbs with ideas that have popped into your head lately.

GOAL!

Anger helps Riley play aggressively in the rink when she needs to. Help Riley get the puck into the goal.

FACE-OFF!

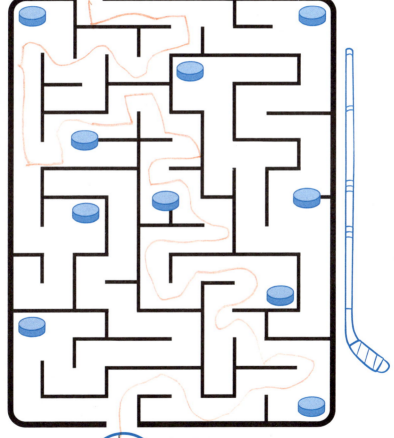

GOAL!

See page 119 for the answer.

Your Islands of
PERSONALITY

Riley's Islands of Personality are what make Riley who she is. What do you think your Islands of Personality look like?

Draw a picture of one of your Islands of Personality.

As Riley gets older, new islands grow.

Draw a picture of an Island of Personality you think you might have five years from now.

CHANGING Minds

Sometimes the Emotions try to remove an idea bulb to get Riley to change her mind.

Write about a time when you changed your mind.

....

....

....

....

....

Now write about a time when you wish you had changed your mind.

....

....

....

....

....

Angry WORDS

The following twelve angry words are hidden in the word search below. Look up, down, across, diagonally, and backward. Can you find them all?

aggravated	fuming	irritated
annoyed	furious	mad
cross	hot	raging
fiery	huffy	sore

```
M Q W E R A G I N G M I K A Z
A T G R C X C G H S O R E Q X
D Y Q N V Z V F J B N U H W C
E U A S I S B D K C H Y G E V
W I S Q B M N S Y R E I F R D
S O Z W N A U A L O G T U T E
D P X H M Q N F P S T R R Y T
E L H E O W M Q O S R E I O A
R K C R P T L W I C E S O P V
F J M T O E O E U X P A U O A
G H I R R I T A T E D Q S I R
H G M Y I R P R Y Z K L R U G
B F L U U D E Y O N N A F Y G
N D O I Y T I T W Q J J D G A
M Y F F U H U Y R A G H X G H
```

How NOT to Ruin Pizza!

Anger knows pizza. Here are a couple of ways to make a simple pizza. Be sure to ask a parent or guardian for permission and help before whipping up any of these recipes!

What You Need:
Sliced English muffin
Toaster oven
Baking sheet
Aluminum foil
Olive oil
Tomato sauce or sliced tomatoes
Shredded mozzarella cheese

Mix It Up
For something different, switch out the muffin and experiment with different types of bread, such as bagels, pita, or flatbread.

What You Do:

1. Ask a parent to help you place the sliced English muffin in the toaster oven for a few minutes so that it is lightly toasted. (It will go in the oven again in a bit, so you don't want to overcook it!)

2. Have your helpful parent or guardian remove the muffin from the toaster.

3. Cover a baking sheet with aluminum foil.

4. Place the English muffin on the baking sheet.

5. Drizzle a little olive oil on top of the muffin.

6. Spread tomato sauce or place sliced tomatoes on top of the muffin.

7. Sprinkle on some shredded cheese.

8. Put the muffin with all its toppings in the toaster oven and heat until the cheese melts. This should take about 5 minutes.

9. Ask a parent or guardian to help you remove the baking sheet from the oven—careful, it will be HOT!

Hit It with Some HEAT

Want to spice up your pizza? Use one of the following spices (or make a blend): cayenne, paprika, chili powder, garlic powder, crushed red pepper. Dash some on your pizza and feel the heat!

Bonus Recipe: SPICY SNACKS

Add some spice to your snacks by using a blend of the above spices. Throw your blend into a sealable bag or container with your snack of choice. Try popcorn, chips, carrots, or cucumbers. Close the bag or container and shake. (This is also a good way to get some frustrations out!) Eat a handful and you may feel like your head is on fire!

RAGE on the Page!

Anger gets enraged when Riley's parents say there will be no dessert. He pushes a lever on the console in Headquarters that causes Riley to throw a tantrum!

Write about a time when you threw a tantrum or got really, REALLY upset.

....

....

....

....

When was the last time you got really angry? What happened? Did you feel better or worse afterward?

....

....

....

....

DOTS of Anger

With a friend, take turns drawing a line to connect two dots below. When a line you draw completes a box, give yourself one point. If Anger is in the box, give yourself two points. When no more boxes can be made, the player with more points wins.

HOCKEY Play

Riley and her parents turn an empty room and a crumpled-up ball of paper into a fun hockey game. If you don't have a big empty space to play in, you can make a miniature ice hockey rink and play anywhere.

What You Need:
Water
A freezer-safe baking dish or pan, at least one
    inch deep
1 plastic berry basket
3 craft sticks
Glue or tape
Scissors
Coins
A button or game piece
Optional: paint or markers

What You Do:
1. Pour water into a freezer-safe dish or pan, filling it so there's about one inch of space to the top.

2. Cut a berry basket in half. Place each half on either side of the pan for goals.

3. Carefully place the pan or baking dish in the freezer and wait until the water is frozen solid.

4. While the water is freezing, use craft sticks to make hockey sticks. Cut a craft stick in half. For each hockey stick, glue or tape one long craft stick and one half craft stick together to form an "L" shape.

5. Decorate the hockey sticks with markers or paint if you like.

6. When the water in the pan is frozen solid (this could take a full day), it's game time!

7. Use your hockey stick to hit the puck (a coin, button, or game piece will work nicely) into the goal. Score!

TIP

If the basket is not heavy enough to stay in place, use some coins to weigh it down.

Anger's
LIKES and DISLIKES

Anger has very strong opinions about . . .
everything! Half of the words on the list below
are things that Anger likes, and half are things
he dislikes. Can you figure out which are which?
Separate the list into likes and dislikes and place
each word in the correct spaces to solve the
crossword puzzles on the following page.
To give you a head start, some of the letters
in the puzzles have been filled in.

WORD BANK:

San Francisco

Spitting

Yelling

Yoga

Aromatherapy

Growling

Fairness

Dessert

Hugs

Injustice

Things Anger **LIKES**

Things Anger **DISLIKES**

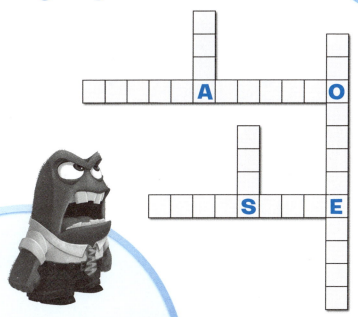

See page 120 for the answers.

Chapter 4

Fear

Operation **Fear**

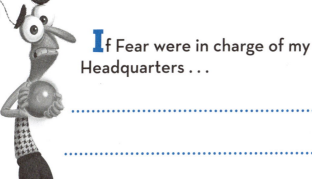

If Fear were in charge of my
Headquarters . . .

....

....

....

....

....

....

....

....

....

....

....

AHHHHH!

Riley's darkest fears are broccoli, Grandma's vacuum, and Jangles the birthday clown. What are your darkest fears?

Make a list here.

1. ....

2. ....

3. ....

4. ....

5. ....

6. ....

7. ....

8. ....

9. ....

10. ....

To Be **FEAR**...

What is Fear thinking?
Fill in the thought bubble below.

Dream DUTY

Fear is not happy when he has to be on Dream Duty and watch Riley's dreams while she sleeps. What did your Emotions see when they were on Dream Duty for you last night?

Draw your dream and write about it here.

(If you don't remember last night's dream, write about the last dream you do remember.)

....

....

....

....

A NEW Home!

Riley and her parents are driving across the Golden Gate Bridge. Help them find their way through the winding streets of San Francisco to their new home!

START

FINISH

See page 121 for the answer.

CREEPY Code

What are some things Fear is afraid of? To find out, replace each letter below with the one that comes before it in the alphabet.

1. **SBJO** ....

2. **GPH** ....

3. **SPMMFS TLBUFT** ....

4. **FBSUIRVBLFT** ....

5. **CFBST** ....

6. **NFUFPST** ....

7. **DPSET** ....

8. **TIBEPXT** ....

9. **QVQQJFT** ....

10. **OPJTF** ....

See page 121 for the answers.

FEAR and FEAR

Which two pictures of Fear match *exactly*?

A

B

C

D

E

F

See page 121 for the answer.

A Rude **AWAKENING**

When Riley has a really bad dream, she wakes up.
Think about a time when you woke up after having
a bad dream.

What was the dream about?

....

....

....

How did you feel when you woke up?

....

....

....

**What did you do after you
woke up?**

....

....

....

Core Memory MATCH-UP

Match each of Riley's core memories on the left to the Island of Personality you think it powers. Draw a line connecting them.

1. Two-year-old Riley dances around the living room wearing nothing but underpants . . . on her head.

Friendship Island

2. Young Riley and her best friend, Meg, make sand castles.

Hockey Island

3. Two-and-a-half-year-old Riley accidentally scores her first hockey goal!

Family Island

4. Young Riley confesses to her parents that she broke a ceramic plate with a hammer.

Goofball Island

5. Riley bakes cookies with Mom and Dad.

Honesty Island

See page 121 for the answers.

My EMOTIONS

Everyone's Emotions and Mind World are unique. What do the Emotions look like inside your Headquarters? Draw them here.
Don't forget to name each one and put a star next to your lead Emotion!

—⌇— NEW Things —⌇—

Riley is nervous about moving to a new city, being in a new home, and going to a new school. When have you experienced something new? What was it like? **Write about it here.**

SCARY School Days

Fear comes up with a long list of things that could go wrong on Riley's first day of school. Stepping in quicksand, spontaneous combustion, and getting called on by the teacher are all on his list.

How many scary things can you come up with?

1. ....

2. ....

3. ....

4. ....

5. ....

6. ....

7. ....

8. ....

9. ....

10. ....

EMBARRASSING Moments

Riley is so embarrassed when she cries in front of the class at her new school. Write about a time when you were embarrassed. What happened? What did you do?

....

....

....

....

....

....

....

....

....

....

My Dream HOUSE

When her family moves, Riley dreams about what her new house in San Francisco will look like. One house is made out of gingerbread, and another comes with a dragon.

Draw a picture of your dream house above.

Chapter 5

Disgust

So Much *Disgust*

If Disgust were in charge of
my Headquarters . . .

....

....

....

....

....

....

....

....

....

....

....

Yuck! EW! Gross!

Soooooo many things disgust Disgust.

Write a list of things that disgust you.

1. ....

2. ....

3. ....

4. ....

5. ....

6. ....

7. ....

8. ....

9. ....

10. ....

DISGUST-Worthy Design

Disgust takes control to help Riley figure out what to wear to school. She says: "When I'm through, Riley will look so good, the other kids will look at their own outfits and barf."

Draw an outfit that Disgust would approve of.

A Tale of THREE EMOTIONS

What's going on between Disgust, Anger, and Fear?
Fill in the comic strip to tell the story.

Disgusting CHARADES

Disgusted faces sure can be fun to make. Get a group of friends together and play Disgusting Charades!

• First, each person should write down a gross situation on a slip of paper. Then fold the slips and put them in a bag. Split up into two teams and get ready to put on your most disgusted faces!

• Next, each person takes a turn pulling out a slip of paper and acting out the "disgusting thing" written on it—without using any words or sounds. Set a timer for 60 seconds. If the player's team can guess what the action is before the timer goes off, they get a point. If the team is unable to guess, the opposing team can score a point if they guess correctly. But they only have one chance to get it right.

• Continue taking turns until you've used all the slips of paper. The team with more points wins!

Here's a list to get you started.

1. Finding a bug in your bowl of cereal

2. Opening a fridge full of rotten fish

3. Drinking a glass of curdled milk

4. Falling into a Dumpster

5. Waking up with a frog on your pillow

GROSS! What IS that?

What do you think Disgust is looking at?

Draw it in the space below.

EMOTIONAL Me

If I were an Emotion, I would be . . .

....

Draw a picture of yourself as an Emotion below.

"EW"

Disgust often thinks . . . "Ew."
How many times can you
find the word "Ew" in the
puzzle below?
Look up, down, across,
diagonally, and backward.

E H J N M V F R J L S W D F V
H G C D R H E M N V E E J S W
W X Q Z U W W N T S W D L Q P
M Y R F E N M K O Y S E X H L
P B H Y W B X O N C B Y D O S
E K F U P U P K L M T R B E W
D W H G M B V Y T E M E P L K
W G F V P D B Y K T W J K M X
E P K L M T G L P O T Y U I V
T H L E W Y H C L I B T C M K
C I N L D R H M O L V G Y K X
E L K B F J U H F G K C D S W
J O F V B N I R D Z B W R K L
D E W P O T G N J L K Y E X A
J P L M B R E D G T O I W T Z

See page 121 for the answer.

And . . . ACTION!

The dream director at Dream Productions directs Riley's dreams. What kind of dream might the dream director in your mind direct?

....

....

....

....

....

....

....

....

....

....

ABSOLUTELY Disgusting

What does Disgust think of the world? It's absolutely disgusting! How many words can you make out of the phrase "absolutely disgusting"?

Here are a few to get you started.

1. ....best..........
2. ....date..........
3. ....suit..........
4. ....
5. ....
6. ....
7. ....
8. ....
9. ....
10. ....
11. ....
12. ....

See page 122 for the answers.

Disgusting MEMORIES

The memory spheres that hold Riley's memories of gross, disgusting, repulsive things are green.

Draw a picture of a time when you felt disgusted.

Test Your TASTE

Disgust is proud of her refined taste. See how your senses of smell and taste compare by playing a taste test game with a friend.
Make sure you and your friend know about any allergies that either of you might have before you play.

What You Need:
Blindfold
Apples, lemons, bananas, peanut butter, chocolate, and marshmallows, or any other foods of your choice
Spoons
Cups or bowls
Paper
Pen or pencil

What You Do:

1. Put a blindfold on the "taster" so she can't see. No peeking!

2. Next, give your friend different foods to try to see if she can guess what each item is.

3. Keep track on a piece of paper to see how many she can identify.

4. Switch places and see how you measure up.

SPICY
Sniff-Test Tip

You can also try conducting a Spicy Sniff test. Instead of tasting different foods, have your friend sniff a variety of spices and herbs. Can she tell ginger from nutmeg?

SNEAKY
Sniff and Taste

For a sneaky taste test, combine the two. Try holding a spice or herb under your friend's nose while she tastes something else. For example, have her eat a slice of apple while sniffing garlic powder. Are you able to trick her senses?

Who's in **CHARGE?**

Answer these questions and follow the path to find out who would be driving your Headquarters if Riley's Emotions were in charge.

If I saw someone cut the line in the cafeteria, I would . . .

Shrug. Who wants to eat gross cafeteria food anyway?

Give them a piece of my mind!

I wish I could . . .

As I take this quiz, I'm . . .

Bubble Wrap the world.

Wondering if I'm going to get dessert after. I deserve it!

Hoping I don't get a paper cut.

ANGER

FEAR

Broccoli **TRAP!**

Disgust does her best to help Riley avoid things she finds gross, such as mice, unfashionable clothing, and broccoli. **Help Disgust get safely through the maze while avoiding the broccoli!**

START

FINISH

See page 122 for the answer.

An **EMOTIONAL** Note

Write a letter to the Emotions that work inside your Headquarters. What would you compliment them on? What might you ask them to do differently?

Dear Emotions,

....

....

....

....

....

....

....

....

....

....

Chapter 6

BING BONG

Imaginary BFF

Riley's imaginary friend Bing Bong is part cat, part dolphin, and part elephant. He's made out of cotton candy with a nougaty center.

Create an imaginary friend of your own and draw him or her here.

ONE-OF-A-KIND Friend

Bing Bong cries candy. Does your imaginary friend do anything extraordinary? Write all about your imaginary friend here.

....

....

....

....

....

Bing Bong flies with Riley in a wagon rocket. How would you and your imaginary friend travel to far-off places?

....

....

....

....

....

Song POWER!

Bing Bong's wagon rocket is powered by his theme song. Fill in the missing words to write a theme song for your imaginary friend.

My friend _____ is my _____ friend
　　　　　　(proper noun)　　　　　　　　　(adjective)

and we love to _____ together.
　　　　　　　　　(verb)

When we _____ with the _____
　　　　　　(verb)　　　　　　　　　　(adjective)

_____ and we _____ and
(plural noun)　　　　　　　(verb)

_____ , we know we'll always be
　(verb)

_____ forever.
(adjective)

It's a JUNGLE Out There!

Help Bing Bong and Riley get to the jungle.

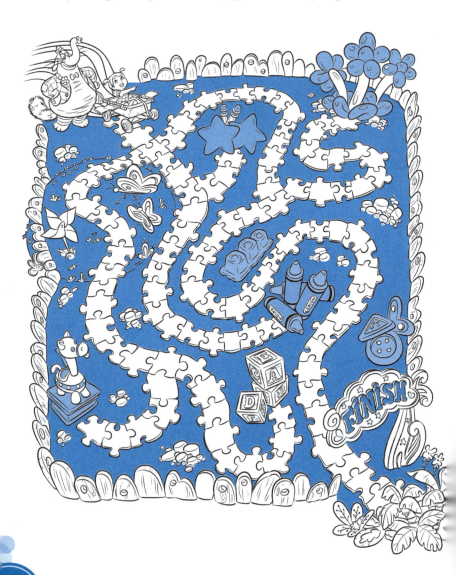

See page 122 for the answer.

Bing Bong's **BAG**

Bing Bong has a bag that can hold anything and everything he puts in it. Hey, why not? It's imaginary!

What would you put inside Bing Bong's bag? Draw some items in his bag below.

SILLY Sport

Bing Bong loves to sing, dance, and act silly. These games will have you and your friends cracking up in no time!

Make Me Laugh

Grab a stopwatch and a friend.

Here are the rules: The first person to sit in the "Serious Seat" has to sit on their hands. Why? Because you can't use your hands to stop yourself from smiling or laughing. That's right, no touching your face!

The "Performer" should start the stopwatch and get ready to act silly. Dance, sing, talk in a wacky voice, tell jokes, or share a funny story—do whatever it takes to make your friend laugh. But keep your hands to yourself. Performers may not touch the person in the "Serious Seat." No tickling allowed!

Then swap places—the person in the "Serious Seat" becomes the "Performer." Whoever makes the person in the "Serious Seat" laugh faster wins!

Silly Songs

All you need for this game is your imagination and your beautiful voice to belt out a tune. Take turns with a friend giving each other a silly word, topic, or idea. That will serve as the song's title. The first person to play makes up a song based on that word or topic—right on the spot. Don't think, just sing! **Here are a few silly topics to get you started:**

1. Stinky Socks

2. The Longest Noodle Ever

3. Pickle Pie

4. Candy Farm

5. A Dog Named Phil

Top TUNES

Record your songs and listen to them after you're done with the game. Who knows? Maybe you have a hit on your hands!

DAYDREAMING

The Train of Thought frequently delivers daydreams to Riley's Headquarters.

Draw a picture of a daydream you would like your Train of Thought to deliver to your Headquarters.

What is Bing Bong thinking?
Fill in the thought bubble below.

FACTS and OPINIONS

Joy and Bing Bong are having trouble sorting the facts from the opinions! Help them by circling "fact" or "opinion" for each statement.

1. Riley plays hockey.
   FACT   **OPINION**

2. Bing Bong cries candy.
   FACT   **OPINION**

3. Song-powered rockets are the best way to get around.
   FACT   **OPINION**

4. Hockey is fun.
   FACT   **OPINION**

5. Imaginary friends should stay around forever.
   FACT   **OPINION**

6. Joy is Riley's lead Emotion.
   FACT   **OPINION**

7. Riley used to live in Minnesota.
   FACT   **OPINION**

8. Pizza in San Francisco is terrible.
   FACT   **OPINION**

See page 123 for the answers.

Seeing DOUBLE

Which two Bing Bongs are *exactly* the same?

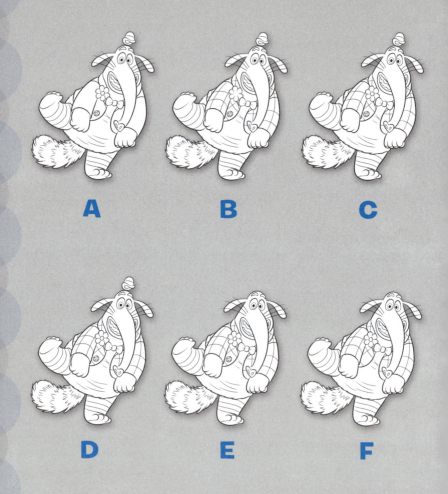

A   B   C

D   E   F

See page 123 for the answer.

Animal **SCRAMBLER**

When Riley was three years old, she loved animals almost as much as she loved Bing Bong!

Unscramble the words to see which animals were Riley's favorites.

OHRES ....

WCO ....

TCA ....

GDO ....

LPHDOIN ....

EALPHETN ....

KDCU ....

BBRITA ....

TLTURE ....

GOFR ....

See page 123 for the answers.

IMAGINATION Land

Imagination Land is Bing Bong's favorite place in Riley's Mind World. Inside Imagination Land are French Fry Forest, Trophy Town, House of Cards, Cloud Town, and Preschool World. And there's always something new being built!

What places would you like to add to Imagination Land? Chocolate Chip Mountain? Puppy Town? Peppermint Stick Park? Storybook Village?

Draw and label some of your own new additions!

Too Much **FUN!**

The following words are missing the letters **F-U-N**.
Place the missing letters in the correct spots to
spell the words.

___ ___ ___N ___Y

___LO ___ ___DER

___ ___N ___EL

___ ___R___ITURE

___ ___ ___D

___ ___R ___ACE

RE___ ___ ___D

___ ___R ___ISH

___L ___ ___G

MA___ ___ ___ACTURE

See page 123 for the answers.

The BING and the BONG

What makes Bing Bong, Bing Bong? Find some of his best qualities in the word search below.

Below is a list of adjectives that describe the exact opposite of Bing Bong. Think of the opposite word for each of the adjectives. Write the word in the space beside the adjective. These will be the words you will search for in the puzzle. Be sure to look up, down, across, diagonally, and backward.

What Bing Bong is NOT:

boring..............................   small ....
serious...........................   common.......................
shy ....   plain.............................
gloomy..........................   vile...............................
sour ....   cruel............................

```
P  L  U  F  R  E  E  H  C
Y  H  A  X  D  S  P  S  O
N  L  I  C  N  J  A  I  L
N  I  M  U  I  K  C  L  O
U  E  G  T  K  H  A  L  R
F  R  I  E  N  D  L  Y  F
X  K  B  E  U  Q  I  N  U
J  C  A  T  E  E  W  S  L
```

See page 123 for the answers.

ANSWER KEY

Page 21:   A and E are the same.

Page 22:

```
F D F G B V D W G J K Z X C V
B O B F D E H C V S W O P N M
L K R V X F R O N C H F R G H
G L O T S A N B C P G F H J Y
N M I R W M H V L K F D G Y T
I N U E E I Y C K O E L F T R
T B Y S R L T X J I D Y F R E
A V T S T Y R U H U F S R D T
K C G E Y K E Z O Y D S I S G
S X B D U M W Q G U G D E C T
I Z S N I N Q W O T C F N W P
U A X W O B A L R R W G D P R
Y Q F R E N C H F R I E S X U
T W O M P V Z A D E Q H F S J
R E L K L C X S E I H P O R T
```

Page 24:

A-4, B-5, C-1, D-2, E-3

Page 25:

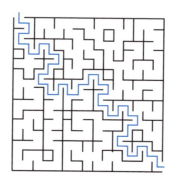

118

Page 35: It makes everything feel droopy.

Page 36: Shadow #5 matches Sadness's shadow.

Page 37:

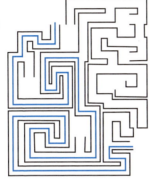

Page 40: 1) memory; 2) fun; 3) foot; 4) cloud; 5) dog; 6) Crying; 7) shortcut; 8) listener

Page 49: Hawaii and San Francisco

Page 51:

Page 55:

```
M Q W E R A G I N G M I K A Z
A T G R C X C G H S O R E Q X
D Y Q N V Z V F J B N U H W C
E U A S I S B D K C H Y G E V
W I S Q B M N S Y R E I F R D
S O Z W N A U A L O G T U T E
D P X H M Q N F P S T R R Y T
E L H E O W M Q O S R E I O A
R K C R P T L W I C E S O P V
F J M T O E O E U X P A U O A
G H I R R I T A T E D Q S I R
H G M Y I R P R Y Z K L R U G
B F L U U D E Y O N N A F Y G
N D O I Y T I T W Q J J D G A
M Y F F U H U Y R A G H X G H
```

Page 63:

Likes:

```
        D E S S E R T
            P
            I
      F     Y T
      A     E T
      I     L I
G R O W L I N G
      N     I N
      E     N G
      S     G
      S
```

Dislikes:

```
          Y
          O
          G
S A N F R A N C I S C O
                      R
              H       O
              U       M
              G       A
    I N J U S T I C E  T
                      H
                      E
                      R
                      A
                      P
                      Y
```

120

Page 69:

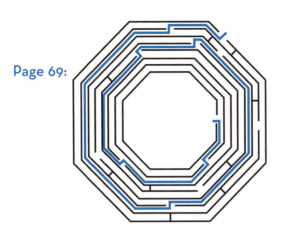

Page 70: rain, fog, roller skates, earthquakes, bears, meteors, cords, shadows, puppies, noise

Page 71: B and D are the same.

Page 73: 1) Goofball; 2) Friendship; 3) Hockey; 4) Honesty; 4) Honesty; 5) Family

Page 90:

```
E H J N M V F R J L S W D F V
H G C D R H E M N V E E J S W
W X Q Z U W W N T S W D L Q P
M Y R F E N M K O Y S E X H L
P B H Y W B X O N C B Y D O S
E K F U P U P K L M T R B E W
D W H G M B V V Y T E M E P L K
W G F V P D B Y K T W J K M X
E P K L M T G L P O T Y U I V
T H L E W Y H C L I B T C M K
C I N L D R H M O L V G Y K X
E L K B F J U H F G K C D S W
J O F V B N I R D Z B W R K L
D E W P O T G N J L K Y E X A
J P L M B R E D G T O I W T Z
```

Note: "Ew" is found 18 times.

Page 92: There are many words that can be made! Some possible answers: all, ate, band, bang, bean, blue, bus, but, dot, egg, end, sand, sang, sea, sob, tiny, toy, tuba, tube, tutu.

Page 98:

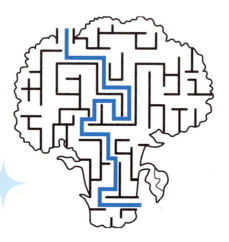

Page 104:

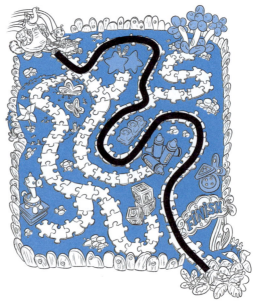

Page 111: 1) fact; 2) fact; 3) opinion; 4) opinion; 5) opinion; 6) fact; 7) fact; 8) opinion

Page 112: C and D are the same.

Page 113: horse, cow, cat, dog, dolphin, elephant, duck, rabbit, turtle, frog

Page 116: funny, flounder, funnel, furniture, fund, furnace, refund, furnish, flung, manufacture

Page 117:
funny
silly
friendly
cheerful
sweet
big
unique
colorful
cute
kind

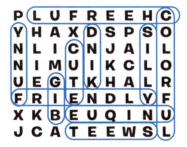

Joy

Find the fun in every day!

Sadness

Goodbyes make me **feel** like a wilted flower.

ANGER
Fight the good fight!

Fear
Be careful and watch out for . . . everything!

125